London Snow

Paul Theroux

London Snow

A Christmas Story

WITH WOOD ENGRAVINGS BY

John Lawrence

Houghton Mifflin Company Boston 1980

P 10 9 8 7 6 5 4 3 2 1

Library of Congress Cataloging in Publication Data

Theroux, Paul.
London snow.

SUMMARY: At Christmas time two orphans and their
guardian search through snowbound London for their
missing landlord, even though he has threatened to
evict them.
[1. Christmas stories. 2. London – Fiction]
I. Lawrence, John, 1933- II. Title.
PZ7.T3524Lo 1980   [Fic]   80-16850
ISBN 0-395-29458-4

I

On this winter afternoon the bright window of the sweet-shop crackled with colour—the red ribbons on a pyramid of chocolate boxes, trays of glazed fruit, marzipan wrapped in crisp green cellophane, and bins of humbugs that shone with an enamelling of sugar. In the centre of the window was a Christmas tree with silver needles, and decorated with baubles of mint lumps and wine gums. It had been raining since morning, but the day had turned cold and the rain-drops had frozen on the shop window, coating it with crystal pebbles that crazed the light and made it merrier.

Two figures, indistinct in the freezing rain, appeared at the corner of Church Road. Behind them, Saint Mary's on the river was a dark steeple against the yellow light from the Chelsea Flour Mill on the far bank. In the middle of the river a black lighter, with the outlines of a barge, was moored to a bobbing barrel. The Old Swan had not yet opened and, closer, The Raven was no more than a swinging sign, cawing in the wind like the black bird painted on it.

Tall and short, the two figures emerged from the crossroads and made their way to the shop. It bulged like an old turret, this last shop in the High Street. *Mutterance & Co.*, said its sign, *All Kinds of Confectionery*. The smaller of the two shadows wore a hooded cape and carried a school satchel. The other was very tall, and in the lamplight his skin was dark silver. The two walked unsteadily, because they were laughing. Their laughter was like a pair of bells pealing, one a low throaty growl, the other small and sweet.

Just as they passed The Raven, a heavy man moved towards the shop and pushed at the door. He was a big man, his shadow a bear on the wall. The door closed behind him, and now he stood hunched before the counter, the wet wool of his shaggy coat dripping.

'Who's that?' The timid voice came from the small hood. It was a girl's voice and it trembled. This was Amy. She peered through the icy window at the dripping coat. Her face was very white and solemn, a tiny triangle with a kittenish concern in the large dark eyes.

'Snyder, from the look of that scruffy coat,' said the other. The voice was a lilting sing-song. This was Wallace. He was tall—twice as big as Amy—and he wore a knitted cap that fit his head like a tea-cosy. Wallace was black. 'I wonder,' he said in his fun-poking voice, 'I wonder what that old monster-man wants.'

They saw the man gesturing in the shop, and they waited. But it was cold outside; December was wrapped darkly around these small streets. It seemed to them that if they walked too far or waited too long they would be swallowed by the London shadows and, groping blindly, become shadows themselves.

A bell rang over the door of the shop as they went in. The man—it was Snyder—turned. His face was all red lumps and bristles, and he was breathless, having just stopped talking. Seeing that it was Wallace and Amy who had come in, he grunted and stamped his wet shoes on the floor.

Behind the counter was an old woman. Her name was Mrs. Mutterance. She was white-haired and small and entirely round. She wore a warm coat and funny fingerless mittens. Her mouth moved constantly. She was sucking a sweet. She said, 'Angels.'

'No more school until January, Ma,' said Amy. 'And that's next year!'

Wallace said, 'It feels like snow.'

'What do you know about snow?' demanded Snyder. 'They don't have snow where you come from.'

'I come from London,' said Wallace.

'Let's say you're not lying through your teeth—which I fancy you are,' said Snyder. 'It hasn't snowed in London since just after the war. Not real snow. Not like we used to have. Drifting over the windows and caving in the roofs. Up to the letter slots in the pillar boxes, it was. You could have skied over to Chelsea and saved the price of a bus fare. Lasted for days, it did, and froze the pipes. Icicles hanging from the drain spouts.' Snyder put his red uneven face close to

Wallace's smooth black face and said, 'It killed people it was so cold. They just froze—they didn't know they were dead. They couldn't help theirselves.'

'Stop that talk,' said Mrs. Mutterance. 'You're trying to scare the boy.'

'I ain't scared,' said Wallace.

Snyder said to Mrs. Mutterance, 'Why, I've seen sleighs in the High Street.'

'It snowed last year,' said Amy.

'That wasn't snow,' said Snyder. 'That was coal dust from the glucose factory and a little sleet. Five minutes later it was raining.'

'It looked like snow,' said Amy.

'You're so small, everything looks like snow. Now don't argue with me. I'm a lot older than you and I know what's what.' Snyder turned to Mrs. Mutterance. 'I didn't come in here to talk about the weather.

Mrs. Mutterance had been working a mint back and forth impatiently in her mouth. She stuttered and then said, 'I've never heard such a lot of old rope in all my life. It's just gas and goose-feathers. You think you were here first, but you weren't. Sleighs in the High Street, indeed! Why, I remember farthings and chamberpots, and you don't hear me boasting to innocent children.'

'The snow was up to here,' said Snyder, punching himself in the chest. 'Years ago.'

But Mrs. Mutterance was not listening to him. She said, 'Your tea's on the table upstairs, my angels.'

Wallace and Amy smiled but did not move.

'Fish paste sandwiches,' said Mrs. Mutterance. Snyder squinted at her. Then he said menacingly to the children, 'I've got business with this lady. Get out unless you want a frashing.'

'This lady is my mum,' said Wallace.

'We know all about it, don't we?' said Snyder.

'She's been my mum almost my whole life.'

'Mine, too,' Amy said, 'Ma, why is Mister Snyder smiling like that?'

'That's no smile,' said Mrs. Mutterance. 'His shoes are too tight.'

'They don't seem to understand that we've got business,' said Snyder.

Mrs. Mutterance said, 'These are my angels. I don't keep secrets from them. Here, have a mint lump and get on with it.'

Snyder would not take the mint lump he was offered. It remained in the knitted palm of the fingerless mittens Mrs. Mutterance wore.

'Take it,' she said. 'It's not a mothball, you know.'

'You might regret you gave me something,' said Snyder. 'After what I've got to tell you.'

'The only thing I shall ever regret,' said Mrs. Mutterance, 'is the disappearance of sixpences.'

'I've got some bad news for you,' said Snyder.

'We used to put them in Christmas puddings,' Mrs. Mutterance explained to Wallace and Amy. 'The sixpences. It was considered lucky if you got one with your helping. Then no one would bring you bad tidings, as this gentleman is about to do. Go on, squire, take this mint lump and say your piece.'

'In that case I'd rather have fudge,' said Snyder.

'I don't do fudge. I've never done fudge. I don't hold with fudge.'

Snyder looked deeply offended.

5

'The mint lump or nothing,' said Mrs. Mutterance. 'And if you don't eat it, I will.'

'Missus,' said Snyder, placing the mint lump on his tongue, 'as you know, I own this entire premises. It is my right to do with it as I wish.'

Wallace set his gaze upon Snyder.

Amy said, 'You're not going to sell the shop!'

'He wouldn't dare,' said Mrs. Mutterance. 'Of course, I know he's a proper City gent, with a piece of rope holding up his trousers, and holes in his shoes for ventilation and moths heaving around in his woolly overcoat. But anyone else wouldn't trust him long enough to get his signature on a contract.'

'I think,' said Snyder confidently, 'that you might be surprised by the extent of my contacts in the world of commerce. As it happens, I have been in consultation with a director of laundry franchises.'

'And his hat leaks,' said Mrs. Mutterance.

Snyder paid no attention to the remark. He said, 'I believe there is a future in washer-dryer operations. I have plans for this 'ere sweet-shop.'

'It's my sweet-shop,' said Mrs. Mutterance.

'Your sweets—my shop,' Snyder said. 'It's going to be a laundry-ette.'

'No!' said Amy.

'A laundry-matic,' said Snyder.

'You can't do that,' said Wallace.

'A washy-teria,' said Snyder.

Mrs. Mutterance swallowed her mint and said fiercely, 'Soap flakes!'

'This is terrible,' whispered Wallace.

But Snyder was still speaking. This was a new Snyder—not the glowering, stamping bear they had known in the past, shouting for the rent money on the first day of the month; not the Snyder who hardly spoke except to say 'Mind my lupins' in the dusty back garden, or 'You're going to come to a sticky end' to Wallace, for no reason the poor boy could name. Sometimes, Snyder would pinch Amy's cheek tightly and when she squawked the old man would say, 'If you ate your greens you wouldn't look like that.' Sometimes, he banged his walking-stick at Kipper the cat and cried, 'You're a devil!' He had plenty of money, but he punished himself with pointless economies: ate chips out of newspaper and beans out of tins to save plates. When he was excited or angry he shouted to Mrs. Mutterance, 'My mother was a saint!'

He lived on the top floor. He was a man of many moods, but happiness was not one of them. And yet this evening, serving an eviction notice on Mrs. Mutterance and her adopted children, he seemed grumpily cheerful and full of strange ideas.

'A modern laundry-ette,' he was saying. 'Washing machines with windows on them, like twenty-four tellies with suds foaming on the screen. They're fun to watch! You can see the bubbles! And over here—'

He walked to the side of the shop. There were jugs of mint imperials and fairy drops on the shelves.

'—some wringers and dryers, all humming busily away. See, those machines don't work unless you put cash money in them.' He whacked a jar of nut clusters. 'I'll put me soap-dispenser here—insert a coin and you get a whole cup of detergent. Maybe I'll knock that wall through to make room for me dry-cleaning machines. They look like tin wardrobes but they bring in the money like billy-o.'

7

'It'll be all machines,' purred Amy sadly.

'Who's talking to you?' said Snyder. Then he added, 'If there's room, I'll put a pot-plant in the window. Maybe a geranium. But the rest will be spick and span.'

'I'm not working in no laundry-ette,' said Wallace.

'No one's asking you to,' said Snyder promptly.

'Well, neither am I,' said Mrs. Mutterance, who had become quite furious. 'Forty years I've been managing this sweet-shop, ever since I was tall enough to see over the counter. We've always had a steady trade, and there's the seasonal items, the Christmas crackers and Easter baskets. I've paid my rent and I've put in my hours. Never absent, never late. I'm not going to stand here sucking a mint while you put in washing machines. I'll never,' she said with dignity, 'turn my back on sweets.'

'There is very little you can do about it, Gertie,' said Snyder. 'This is my building, not yours.' He opened his mouth wide and said, 'I owns it!'

'I'll have no part of it,' said Mrs. Mutterance. 'See how smartly you run your laundry-ette with no one behind the counter.'

'The beauty of a laundry-ette,' said Snyder, 'is that there is no counter. You will not be required.'

'Rumples—um-plums—um-rambasher!' said Mrs. Mutterance, choking with rage.

'The beauty of a laundry-ette,' said Snyder, 'is that people puts money in a machine and then puts in their clothes. They takes out their clothes, but they leaves their money. That is done by the guv'nor, missus. *I* takes out their money.'

'Merdle,' said Mrs. Mutterance.

'The work is done by the customer,' said Snyder. 'I provides the facilities.'

'Forty years,' said Mrs. Mutterance.

'I was in the army then,' said Snyder. 'I wouldn't know about that, I had the war to occupy me. I was being fired at in anger.'

'The buzz-bombs fell on Battersea,' said Mrs. Mutterance. 'The air was thick with them some nights. You had to sleep in the shelter, or under the stairs. Plaster fell on you. The windows cracked. You waited for the "all clear" and then you carried on humping jars of sweets from the basement.'

The children watched in alarm.

'I was in the war,' said Mrs. Mutterance.

'If that is so,' said Snyder, 'why is it that I collect an army pension and you don't?'

This was a fact. Every Thursday, Snyder went over to Chelsea to collect his money. Snyder walked the mile from the corner of Church Road, across Battersea Bridge to the pension office. 'Keeps me fit,' he said. But he was too mean to pay for the bus.

'Just think,' said Snyder, 'the whole shop will be white lino and shiny machines. And out front the coat of arms—"By Appointment to Her Majesty the Queen, Launderers and Dry Cleaners." '

'Codswallop,' said Mrs. Mutterance.

'Come over here, missus,' said Snyder.

But Mrs. Mutterance did not move. Snyder was smiling out of the window, wheezing with satisfaction. Across the frozen square, on the corner of Vicarage Crescent and the High Street, a brick building bore the gold and blue shield, 'By Appointment to Her Majesty the Queen, Office Cleaning Specialists.'

'Her Majesty's got offices,' said Snyder, 'and Her Majesty's got clothes. And the royal clothes need washing as much as ours do.'

'Yours especially,' said Wallace.

'You,' said Snyder, 'are going to come to a sticky end.' He jammed a cloth cap onto his head, but before he stepped out into the freezing rain he said, 'Now I will be on my way. But remember—Christmas is coming. Rent's due early. I'll expect it Saturday. Take my advice,' he went on, 'and use the holiday period to find yourselves some new premises.'

'I hope he falls in the river,' said Wallace, twisting his hands in anger.

Mrs. Mutterance was too stunned to reply. They went upstairs, and she watched Wallace and Amy have their tea—and she listened for the bell, which meant that a customer had entered the shop. But there were no customers in this icy gale. They could hear the river crashing at the embankment: it was like an ocean's surf. At six, Mrs. Mutterance went down and locked the shop door.

Wallace and Amy heard Snyder pacing in his room upstairs. That odd choking and whistling noise was Snyder singing—he was happy.

'He's evil,' said Wallace.

'I don't think he's evil,' said Amy. 'I think he's a bad man.'

'That's the same thing,' said Wallace.

'No, it's not,' said the small girl. 'Evil people never change, but bad ones sometimes do.'

'Do you think that old monster will change?'

Amy said nothing. She had started to cry.

Normally, at nightfall, Wallace told Amy a ghost

story, using as his characters the people whose names were written on the memorial windows and the grave-stones at Saint Mary's. Wallace said they haunted the neighbourhood—Nathaniel Potticary, the Stringers, Roper, the clubfooted Whickman, and the strangest one of all, whom Wallace said had been a spy two hundred years ago, Benedict Arnold: his bones lay beneath the church.

There were no ghost stories tonight. Snyder's sudden visit had terrified them sufficiently. Amy wept softly, and Wallace sat on his hammock with his hands on his knees.

When Mrs. Mutterance came upstairs to have her own tea, Amy asked in a pleading voice, 'Where will we go?'

Mrs. Mutterance blinked and said sadly, 'Goolistan. Or Nether Wallop. Or the Rinks of Merrivale. Oh, ain't the old cruel!'

II

Towards midnight, in his hammock in the hall, Wallace was woken by silence. Such a soundlessness ensued, he could hear no more than his own lungs, and it was then he became worried. He waited in the darkness. There would be a plane soon: the sweet-shop was on the flight-path—planes flew low over the High Street and continued down York Road to London Airport.

Wallace listened for the whirling thunder and gusts of a jet engine. There was nothing. A train? They often shuddered from one wall to the other, seeming to vibrate invisibly across his hammock; and at night they brayed as they approached Clapham Junction. Even a distant train was near in the dark of night. But there was no train, and none of the noises that had reassured him in the past. The city did not throb. It lay mournful and deadened, as if made out of cloth, and the only sound was the squeak of his hammock-rope on the hook.

'Stop pendling, Wally.'

It was Mrs. Mutterance, groaning from her room at the end of the hall.

'Sorry, Ma.'

He lay still in his hammock, frightened by the silence of the city.

'Are you asleep, boy?'

'Yes, Ma. Sound asleep.'

'Just stop your pendulation.'

Mrs. Mutterance had been woken by a bad dream. In this dream she was sitting on packing cases and tea chests in the High Street. There were sweets going stale in the packing cases, and clothes stiffening into wrinkles in the tea chests. The shop was shut and Mrs. Mutterance had nowhere to go. Wallace and Amy watched from the kerb. There was not a sound or a voice of any kind to be heard, and she was very cold. The dream was a dream, but the silence was real, and so was the cold. And now, awake, all she heard was the squeak of Wallace's hammock-rope. Mrs. Mutterance did not find the silence strange. It was not emptiness; it was like an unformed thought, a blurred memory of something she could not recall clearly. She could not say what this memory was. But certain words came to her: Trood, and gob-stoppers, and sleighing on a tea tray.

Amy heard voices—Mrs. Mutterance's and Wally's. She slept curled like a kitten, and the big-eared Burmese kitten, Kipper, slept beside her, with its nose between its paws. Amy did not stir. She opened her eyes and stared into Kipper's yellow eyes. Kipper yawned and went back to sleep. Amy sniffed the silence, and did the same. She did it by putting her head down and deliberately seeming to dive, and then falling through silence, slowly turning. Sleep, for Amy, was an experience of empty space: she left the ledge of wakefulness by her pillow and made a long drop through sleep, arriving in the morning with a soft bump, slightly startled, in her own bed. But Amy too had had a curious feeling about waking that night, for the night in her room had been as quiet as her dreams.

The morning for the children was like no other morning they had known. There were no city noises —not even dogs. No planes, no cars, no trains. There had been times when a motor launch on the river would hoot in the early morning as it passed Saint Mary's and The Old Swan. There were no hoots. And the sky was still. It was as if London were holding its breath.

Wallace opened his eyes. It was dark in the hall; his nose was very cold. Mrs. Mutterance looked at her alarm clock—it was past eight! Amy woke without moving, hearing Mrs. Mutterance cry, 'My bedsocks are rucked!'

Then Amy saw the street-lamps of Church Road— their yellow froth in the grey air. And there was another colour: it was an eerie blue fluorescence, and when she looked again she saw a gigantic line of laundry, like sheets on a rope, hanging over Vicarage Crescent. She heard the clank of milk bottles—that was odd, because she had not heard the engine of the milk van. Why was the milkman walking, and why didn't his footsteps make a sound?

'What's wrong, Ma?' asked Wallace.

Mrs. Mutterance was in her dressing gown and red bedsocks. She wore her fingerless mittens and she was standing at the kitchen door clawing gently at her scalp.

'I've got something on my mind,' she said.

'Snyder?' asked Wallace.

'No. Just now I thought I was ten years old. I was Trood.'

Wallace began to laugh. He had a growling laugh, and he shut his eyes and nodded as the laughter rolled out of him.

'That's what my father called me—Trood. He gave me gob-stoppers from the shop. I used to slide down the hill near the flats on a tea-tray. I must have been ten—to get myself onto a tea-tray.'

It was the morning that made her think of it. She had not known a morning like this for fifty years. It was the silence and the snow, and the cold, too. It was dry; there was no dampness in it, and no wind; just the still white scarf of winter.

Wallace said, 'I dreamed that London was made out of cloth.'

Amy said, 'I can see laundry everywhere!'

'Don't say that,' said Mrs. Mutterance. 'It reminds me of Snyder's washy-teria.'

Wallace said, 'Cottonwool!'

It was snow.

It clung thickly to the rooftops where it was nearly blue. It was mounded like white eyebrows above the windows of the houses, and it had blown against the brick walls and stuck, making beards hang from the sills. It was piled against the doors and made caps on the tops of lamp-posts. Each spike on the churchyard

15

fence was encased in a fluffy sheath, and so far the only marks in the white street—what a beautiful street it seemed!—were the milkman's footprints.

Mrs. Mutterance, Wallace and little Amy stood at the front window above the shop and marvelled. The city had a new shape, very soft contours and different colours. It was hardly a city. The Chelsea Flour Mill across the river had become a snowy mountain, and behind it was a landscape of larger and smaller hills. It was as if, in the night, the city had been removed and in its place an empty countryside of simple hills had appeared.

Saint Mary's seemed a country church, banked by snow, at the edge of a snowy meadow where lambs nestled. But the meadow was the frozen river on which the snow had settled, and some icy wavelets had produced the illusion of lambs. The city was simplified. It was perfectly dry and white. And this, Mrs. Mutterance said, was what had woken them in the night: the covering of snow had shut out every sound, stopped the trains, grounded the planes, kept everyone indoors. Even now, in the morning, there was no movement. The city lay frozen and very still. The birds were gone, there were no voices, the sky was empty. The nearer warehouses were mountainous and their chutes were like ski-slopes. The wreckage on the patch of waste ground near Westover Road was gone, and in its place were bulging igloos and whitened statuary. The window panes were feathery from the flakes that had stuck to them, and from every eave and drainpipe hung icicle daggers and the loveliest swords of ice.

'Why is it so quiet, Ma?' asked Amy.

'The snow's stopped the yip-yap,' said Mrs. Mutterance. 'It's a kind of clogulation—it just came down and snuffled everything. Gosh, ain't it pretty?'

'It's all smothered up,' said Wallace.

'But where's the river, Ma?'

'It's not on top anymore,' said Mrs. Mutterance. 'My guess is that it's underneath.'

There was no traffic on the river. They were used to seeing it as black and spiky at high tide, grey and swift at low tide, churning in all directions when the tide was rising. Rowers in narrow skiffs often slid along the river, like water insects. The river had enlarged the city by mirroring it, but now its size had diminished. There were no reflections, only an even whiteness which matched the silence. The wet black city was gone.

'There's a house on top, where the river should be,' said Wallace.

It was the lighter, transformed to a shed. It did not bob, and the snow had drifted round it. Its bow was covered, its portholes at the level of the snow, and the drum on which it was moored was hidden. Closer, the masts on the Thames sailing barges at Saint Mary's embankment were like frozen trees.

Amy said, 'It's magic.'

'No,' said Mrs. Mutterance, 'it's about as normal as it could be. Normal and thermal. But take a good look now, because pretty soon it will waterfy and go down the drains. You know, this is what London was like when I was a girl, and we had silver sixpences in the Christmas pud. Goodness, it takes me back! I had my own tea-tray, for sliding. My father gave me glacier mints and called me Trood.'

She spoke dreamily: she had recovered her happiness. There was no mention of Snyder.

Wallace said, 'I'm glad there's no school. We can get some tea-trays and go sliding.'

'Hurry,' said Mrs. Mutterance. 'This weather won't last—and it *is* weather that London has, not a climate. With a climate you know what it's going to be like tomorrow, but with weather you don't know whether it is or not. Maybe that's why they call it weather.'

Still looking out of the window, Amy said, 'Richard hasn't gone out.'

'How do you know?' said Wallace.

She pointed to the doorway across the crescent. 'No footprints.'

'Clever stick,' said Mrs. Mutterance.

'And Plastic Jacket hasn't gone to work,' said Amy, pointing to another doorway, the home of a man whose jacket squeaked.

'Maybe he's afraid of freezing to death,' said Wallace.

'It looks cold enough for that,' said Mrs. Mutterance. 'Ever see anything so white? Murderously pretty, it is.'

'I wish Snyder would go out,' said Wallace. 'And freeze to death.'

'That's a bastable and harrowing thing to say!'

'I'd like to steal his mittens and take the paper out of his shoes,' said Wallace. Mr. Snyder lined his shoes with the *Daily Mail* in the winter to plug the holes. 'And put more leaks in his hat. Then they'd find him flat on his back, as stiff as a fish finger.'

'Apologise!' cried Mrs. Mutterance.

'Sorry, Ma,' said Wallace, but he was smirking at the window as he did so.

'Even if he is going to kick us into the street, you shouldn't say that. You should feel sorry for his stupidity. The man's a moggy—he doesn't know any better. The trouble with Snyder is that he carries his own world around with him, and he doesn't want us in it.'

Over breakfast, Mrs. Mutterance switched on the radio. London had had its worst snowfall for fifty years, said the announcer. The trains had been cancelled, the airport was closed, the buses could not run. The chimes of Big Ben were silenced by the frost which had stilled the hammers. A skier had been seen in Park Lane, and for the first time in recent memory the Thames had frozen over.

'We knew that, didn't we?' said Mrs. Mutterance. She stood up. 'Time to open the shop.'

'But there won't be any customers,' said Wallace.

'Duty,' said Mrs. Mutterance.

'Isn't it pretty?' said Amy. 'I don't want anyone to go outside and spoil it with footprints.'

'Have your fun while you can,' said Mrs. Mutterance. 'There are two tea-trays in the cupboard. Mark my words, the snow will be gone before nightfall.'

It was a very short day. After lunch it began to grow dark, but still the snow lay thick on the houses, still the river remained frozen, and the city still looked white and countrified, simpler than they had ever seen it.

Mrs. Mutterance stayed in the shop, wearing her coat and hat and fingerless mittens. Wallace and Amy took their tea-trays to Battersea Bridge Road—and they walked in the middle of the road. Snowploughs had begun to clear some roads, but it was so cold the snow remained in great piles, where it had been shifted, making canyons along the kerbs. There were no cars, and most of the shops were closed. The only people Wallace and Amy saw were children, who told them that the best place to slide was down Latchmere Hill. The children had squares of linoleum or strips of cardboard or, like Wallace and Amy, tea-trays.

It was dark at three-thirty, and as quiet as midnight. When Wallace and Amy got back to the shop, Mrs. Mutterance greeted them and said that not a single soul had been in all day. There were some tyre tracks in the crescent, but the ploughs had not come to this small corner of London. So Wallace and Amy thought they were saved, and if it stayed cold there would be snow tomorrow. It was like a foreign country, and they liked it.

'I had a little time on my hands,' said Mrs. Mutterance, 'I nipped upstairs and made you some Wet Nelly. You can have it after your tea.'

She walked to the window and said softly, 'It's going to be harrowing tomorrow.'

'You mean the snow will be gone?' said Wallace.

'No, sir. Tomorrow I hand over the rent money for the last time. Then, you and me and these sweets will have to find a new stall. That's the whole truth. But there's nothing to be done about it, so let's say no more.'

'I'm not going to think about that,' said Amy. 'I'm just going to think about the snow.'

'The most beautiful thing,' said Mrs. Mutterance, 'is that London snow is like every other kind of snow. Now, I find that reassuring, don't you?'

III

That night there was a new fall of snow. The city was whitened further, but it was less cold than it had been. The freezing temperatures of the previous day had not lasted. The snow, more like insulation, was bluer and stickier. Large wet flakes were still falling at dawn. Although the city remained quiet, Big Ben's chimes had begun to ring again. And now it did not seem so strange that no buses could be heard and no trains were running and few people were out. The London snow had altered the city. London was snowy roofs and smoking chimneys, muffled voices and pale bony light.

Wallace said, 'I'd be happy, except for one thing.'

Amy said, 'What will we do?'

Mrs. Mutterance had been stirring porridge. Lost in reflection, she let go of the wooden spoon. The porridge had become so thick the spoon remained standing upright, with heavy bubbles breaking all around it in the pan.

'I'm handing over the rent money today,' said Mrs. Mutterance. 'To Bean-wit.' That was one of the names she had given Snyder. 'Hollop', 'Rattler', 'Brandish' and 'Buckets' were others. He lived just above them and could hear every word they said, so she used these secret names in order that the old man would not know she was whispering against him.

'Make him wait for it,' said Wallace.

'I've always paid on time,' said Mrs. Mutterance. 'I'll give it to him this afternoon, when he gets back from his pension. Pension! Rent! The man's as rich as a lord! But let's start the day right and not talk about Bean-wit.'

'What will we do?' said Amy, in the same mournful voice.

'Play in the snow,' said Mrs. Mutterance. 'You might never see snow again in this city. You'll have something to tell your grandchildren. Play, my angels, and forget about this business with'—she raised her eyes to the ceiling—'Lord Hollop.'

The porridge was as stiff as paste and lumpy, but Wallace and Amy ate it obediently. Fussing would only have made them sadder.

They went out. They found slippery hills and four-foot drifts. They saw that the pillar boxes lay half-buried. The snow was wet, and soon they were wet. They did not mind. They forgot about their lunch and spent the day sliding down the hills and playing in the snow. They tried not to think that within a week they would have no house and no shop and would be thrown into the cold and the snow by Snyder. But there might not be snow for long. A thaw had begun: they knew it when they saw how, where the winter sunlight had struck the river, the ice had darkened. There were cracks in it, like the veins in marble, and black holes near where the lighter was moored in midstream.

Mrs. Mutterance was waiting for them when they returned to the shop. On her face was an expression of puzzlement, hope and fear, which she voiced in the word, 'Wonderfright.'

Wallace said, 'Hi, Ma.'

Mrs. Mutterance said, 'He's gone.'

'Who's gone?'

'Buckets—Rattler—Bean-wit.' Then she realised there was no need for secrecy. 'Snyder,' she said.

Wallace said, 'Beautiful!'

'Don't shout, boy. I went up there and knocked. I've been knocking all afternoon. He didn't come back.'

'He's just late—I'm sure of it,' said Amy.

Mrs. Mutterance said, 'He's never been late before.'

'It's never snowed like this before.'

'It's snowed,' said Mrs. Mutterance.

'I know he'll be back,' said Amy.

Saying so, she cocked her head to the side and listened for the tramping shoes of Snyder on the stairs. There was no sound, though a cold shadow seemed to press upon the window pane. They looked that way and saw that night had fallen.

Wallace said, 'Maybe he froze!'

'Wally!' said Mrs. Mutterance. 'That's an evil thought.'

'He's an evil man.'

Mrs. Mutterance wheezed, 'He hain't hall heevil,' and then coughed.

'But he's bad, Ma,' said Amy.

Mrs. Mutterance seemed unsure of this. 'He's doing what he thinks is the right thing,' she admitted. 'And I think it's the wrong thing.'

'If he's lost,' said Wallace, 'he ain't doing anything. I hope he stays lost.'

'I know what you mean, Wally,' said Mrs. Mutterance. 'But we're obliged. We're the only ones who know he's lost. We might have to report him missing.'

'Let's eat and forget about him,' said Wallace.

'Let's look at his room for clues,' said Mrs. Mutterance. 'If we don't find any, we'll eat.'

They went to Snyder's room, climbing in single file up the narrow staircase. The door was not locked. They walked in—but fearfully: perhaps he had slipped back into the room? He might stand up and howl at them for intruding. He was not inside. But each of them knew that something was wrong. The drawers were yanked out as if someone had been rifling them. The floor was littered with paper and rags. The oil lamp was tipped over. And the bed was a horrible sight, piled high with horse blankets and old newspapers.

For several anxious seconds they thought that Snyder, dead or alive, might be lying beneath this mess on the bed—it was humpy enough to contain a man. But Wallace kicked the bed and said, 'Anyone there?' There was no reply. He prodded it with a broom handle, but the broom handle sank into the pile. Wallace said, 'He's not underneath.'

'Look,' said Amy. She pointed to a rag on the floor. It was covered with blood.

'Muddy blurter!' Mrs. Mutterance said. 'Phone

the police! Don't touch anything—they'll want to check for footprints. Drop that broom handle, Wally —they'll think you're accomplished!'

Mrs. Mutterance panted down to the shop and dialled the emergency number. Moments later she was saying, 'I want to report a blurter—a mincing— a murder, that's right—'

When the policeman arrived, Mrs. Mutterance said, 'Now that constable looks as though he means business. Look at that mackintosh. Look at that helmet. A push-bike, as well.' The policeman had a black beard and his face was red. There was snow in his beard: he had pedalled some distance. He greeted Mrs. Mutterance and then spoke into a pocket radio-transmitter. 'Hoskins at Vicarage Crescent, Batter-sea. Corner of Church Road. The sweet-shop.' There was a crackle of confirmation, and then he said, 'Will report details shortly, over.'

'It's upstairs,' said Mrs. Mutterance.

'You stay down here,' said the policeman to Wallace and Amy. He was firm without being rude. With a great deal of flapping and folding he removed his mackintosh.

'They've already seen the tragedy,' said Mrs. Mutterance. 'I don't keep secrets from them.'

Upstairs, the policeman entered the room cau-tiously, with a torch in one hand and his truncheon in the other. Mrs. Mutterance pushed ahead of him and switched on Snyder's bottle lamp, apologising as she did so for leaving fingerprints on it. 'But I'm sure there are footprints and fingerprints all over the place. Ever see such a mess in all your career? This is the scene of the crime—no doubt about that.'

The policeman said, 'Where's the body?'

'There's no body,' said Mrs. Mutterance. 'Don't bother to look for a body here. We looked already and didn't find one. Wally even thumped the bed. If you find some fingerprints on that broom handle I expect they'll be Wally's. But he's innocent of any crime or wrongdoing. He was in the snow at the time—'

Interrupting her, the policeman said, 'If there's no body, how do you know there's been a murder?'

'Heavydence,' wheezed Mrs. Mutterance.

The policeman smiled.

'Show the constable what we found, Wally.'

Wallace picked his way across the littered room and solemnly pointed with his long black finger at the gory rag.

Now the policeman became interested. He crouched and stroked his beard and looked closely at it. Then he held it near the lamp.

'Are you sure you know what you're doing, constable?' asked Mrs. Mutterance in disbelief. 'There might be fingerprints on that. Hairs. Crumbs. Telltale wrinkles. Clues of all kinds.'

'Under the circumstances,' said the policeman, 'that's a risk I'm willing to take.'

'I expect you'll want to send it to the laboratory.' Mrs. Mutterance turned to Wallace and Amy. 'For tests, see. They'll have to run tests on this whole room. The mess it's in, I wouldn't want their job!'

But the policeman had dropped the sticky rag.

'What about the blood then?' said Wallace.

'Ketchup,' said the policeman, sourly.

'The filthy pig must have been eating his fish and

26

chips in here!' said Mrs. Mutterance. 'Thank goodness it's not blood. I was beginning to feel a bit queer.'

'I'll be off,' said the policeman, and started for the door.

'Just a minute, constable,' said Mrs. Mutterance. 'I want to report a disappearance.'

'Yes?' The policeman took out a pencil and pad.

'The occupant of this room has vanished,' said Mrs. Mutterance. 'He might be the victim of foul play.'

'When did you see him last?'

'I heard him banging about yesterday.'

'You didn't see him?'

'Banging about is as good as seeing him. Then, he left the house today and that was the last we knew. He never came back.'

'Do you know where he was going?' asked the policeman, making a note on his pad.

'Oh, yes. To collect his pension. In Chelsea.'

'Has it occurred to you,' said the policeman, 'that he might have missed his bus?'

'Has it occurred to you, constable, that there are no buses running in London? I am surprised by your lack of conduction.'

'He'll be back,' said Wallace. 'I just know it.'

'You sound as if you'll be sorry to see him,' said the policeman.

'We will,' said Wallace.

'Don't pay any attention to him, constable—the boy's upset.' Mrs. Mutterance went close to the policeman and said, 'A man has vanished. Doesn't matter what sort of man. We've got to find him.'

The policeman had been amused, then bewildered,

hen suspicious. Now he looked annoyed. He lifted his pad and said, 'Can you give me his name?'

'Bean-wit,' said Mrs. Mutterance. 'I mean—'

'Bristleface,' said Wallace.

'The giant,' said Amy.

'Stop this!' said Mrs. Mutterance. 'His name's Snyder. Reginald Snyder.'

'Reginald?' said Wallace. 'I never knew his name was Reginald!'

The policeman glared at Wallace, who was laughing. 'Physical characteristics,' said the policeman. 'What does he look like?'

'Like a bear,' said Wallace, 'a toothless bear.'

'He's taller than me,' said Amy. 'And he smells.'

Mrs. Mutterance said, 'Yes, he's rather elderly, but frankly he's so bastable and harrowing you'd never notice his age. Oh, the old can be cruel, there's no doubt of that.'

'How was he dressed?'

'Like a tramp,' said Wallace.

'He has holes in his shoes,' said Mrs. Mutterance. 'The shoes themselves are brown. Leather. Of a sort often worn by a man his age. Also his hat leaks.'

'Can you tell me anything about his habits'

'He's stingy and mean,' said Amy.

'He kicked Kipper,' said Wallace. 'He's kicking us out, too. Right into the road, so he can turn the sweet-shop into a laundry-ette.'

'We have nowhere to go,' said Amy. 'What will we do?'

'My children are upset,' said Mrs. Mutterance.

The policeman showed his incredulity by nibbling on the end of his pencil. 'These are your children?'

28

'Indeed they are, constable. Have been for years. As for Reginald Snyder, I would prefer not to comment on his habits.'

'But you say he disappeared,' said the policeman. 'Did he have any enemies that you know of?'

'Mannyfold,' said Mrs. Mutterance. 'Which is why I suggest you catch him—I mean, find him. Before he falls into the hands of his enemies and they give him a well-deserved thrashing.'

The policeman had stopped writing on his pad. 'I doubt that we can do anything about this,' he said. 'With all respect, Madam, I suggest that you are wasting my time.'

'A man's life is at stake,' said Mrs. Mutterance. 'He's lost in the snow.'

'And how long did you say he's been gone?'

'I should say, since lunchtime.'

The policeman smiled. He put his pad and pencil away. He went downstairs and slipped on his mackintosh and bicycle clips. Then he said, 'I'm a good-natured fellow, but this joke has gone too far. Of course, I will file my report, and let's hope he's come to no serious harm. But I'm sure this Snyder, wherever he is, will be able to look after himself. You shouldn't worry about him.'

'I'm not worried about him,' said Mrs. Mutterance. 'I'm worried about us.'

'You haven't got a thing to worry about,' said the policeman, and with that, he mounted his bicycle and wobbled through the slippery snow towards The Raven.

'It's no use,' said Mrs. Mutterance, 'we're completely debunked. And what with all this yip-yap, the only thing left to eat in the larder is bread and scrape.'

IV

'We'll have to find him ourselves,' said Mrs. Mutterance gloomily. 'I'd hoped it wouldn't come to this. I wanted to turn the whole matter over to the police, but that constable was no help. Such a nice chap, really, but he didn't try very hard, did he?'

'I think he knew old Bean-wit wasn't worth looking for,' said Wallace.

'It's five o'clock,' said Mrs. Mutterance. 'There's still time.'

'Let's do it tomorrow,' said Wallace.

Mrs. Mutterance said, 'By then it might be too late.'

Wallace looked at Amy and giggled. 'That's what I was hoping!'

'I don't like your attitude, Wally. It's cruel.'

'He wanted to get rid of us, Ma,' said Wallace. 'But now he's been got rid of. Don't you see? We'll be saved if he doesn't come back. We'll have the shop and the flat and the house and everything will be all right.'

'We won't have to go,' said Amy.

'If we don't look for him, he'll be lost,' said Mrs. Mutterance. 'Do you want that harrowing thing on your conscience?'

Wallace stood up and said loudly, 'I'd rather have him on my conscience than tramping around upstairs in this house!'

Amy said, 'Someone else can look for him, can't they?'

'Impossible,' said Mrs. Mutterance. She blew out her cheeks. 'Infictious. Out of the question. Pure flapdoodle.'

'Why?' asked Wallace.

'No one will look for him.' She shook her head. 'He's too bastable. No one wants to see him again.'

'You admit it!' said Wallace, thumping the table with his dark fist.

'Yes. But that's why we have to look.' Mrs. Mutterance spoke slowly. 'Because no one else will.'

'It's too cold for a search party,' said Wallace.

'How cold do you think he feels?' said Mrs. Mutterance.

'He deserves to suffer,' said Wallace.

'If he suffers he's human. And if he's human he's worth saving,' said Mrs. Mutterance.

'I don't want to do it,' said Amy. 'I agree with Wally.'

'We have no choice,' said Mrs. Mutterance. 'But before we go we need a few theories as to what might have happened to him.'

'I think he was being horrid to someone,' said Amy.

31

'And the person shoved him into a snowbank. And he's still there.'

'Foul play is certainly a matter of factibility,' said Mrs. Mutterance. 'What do you say, Wally?'

'My theory is, he was walking along and saw a bottle cap in the snow. He thought it was a shilling. He bent over to pick it up and fell on his bonce.'

'Sherbet,' said Mrs. Mutterance, pondering this. 'Rubious.'

'What's your theory, Ma?' asked Amy.

'That he went out and got lost,' Mrs. Mutterance said, gravely straightening her mittens. 'And I think we should go and find him.'

They went out and, separately, they searched for Snyder. Mrs. Mutterance walked to Battersea Bridge, but before she had got halfway across it she noticed something odd: the river was no longer frozen. It was black with rustling waves, and in its current were broken segments of ice tumbling towards Vauxhall. She noticed, too, that the air had become less cold—certainly the river had thawed and it seemed fuller and blacker than it had ever been. But the snow on the banks and the snow on the bridge and the rooftops was still there, yellowing in the lamp light. She could hear the whisper of the current, the crisp sound of the ice chunks chipping against each other in the whirlpools around the pillars of the bridge, and coursing past the lighter on its bobbing barrel. She walked as far as Chelsea, but the pension office was closed. There was nothing she could do but turn back.

Wallace sauntered in the High Street with Amy. They were still not sure whether they wished to find

Snyder, and at every dark alley-way Wallace said in a low voice, 'Are you in there, you old monster-man?' They bought a Christmas candle and looked at toys in the shop windows. After the shops closed, they went home.

'Not a sign of him,' said Wallace to Mrs. Mutterance, when they returned to their home over the sweet-shop.

'No,' said Mrs. Mutterance in a faraway voice.

A plane went overhead, the first plane for days. They heard it travel down York Road towards Wandsworth Bridge and the power station. And the trains had started shunting and hooting at Clapham Junction.

'The river's unfreezing. The snow will be gone soon,' said Mrs. Mutterance.

'At least we looked for Beanie,' said Wallace.

'But we didn't want to find him,' said Mrs. Mutterance. 'That's why we didn't find him. Our theories were no good.'

It was nearly bedtime. Mrs. Mutterance made cups of cocoa, and as they were sitting at the kitchen table drinking them, Wallace said, 'I don't see why it's our job to find him. He's the last man in the world I want to see. Even the police don't want to see him. They know what sort of monster-man he is.'

'But we're the only people who can find him,' said Mrs. Mutterance.

'I don't like him,' said Amy.

'That is correct, but it's not right,' said Mrs. Mutterance. 'If you don't like a person, you can't find him. But if you know him and sympathise with him you'll have no trouble at all. I think if we really try to sympathise with him we'll know what became of him. Let's try. Ready? Put your cocoa down and sympathise!'

They bowed their heads as if they were praying, and for several minutes there was silence at the table. Finally, Wallace spoke.

'I can't,' he said. 'I'm trying, but I just can't—I hate him too much.'

'Amy?' said Mrs. Mutterance. 'Can you imagine what it would be like to be Snyder?'

Amy's eyes were shut. She said, 'Yes. Big and horrid. So heavy he can hardly lift his feet.'

Mrs. Mutterance pressed her fingerless mittens together and kept her eyes tightly shut. 'It's no good,' she said. 'We've got to try harder.' Then she opened her blue eyes and relaxed and said, 'I know. Instead of thinking about Snyder, we'll think about ourselves. We'll try to pretend that each of us is Snyder.'

'Yuck,' said Wallace.

'No, go on,' said Mrs. Mutterance. 'Pretend you're Snyder—just for a minute. Now, if I was Snyder, what would I do?' She shut her eyes again and after a moment she said, 'He got fed up.'

Wallace was making conjuring motions with his hands. He said, 'He didn't put enough clothes on. He was in a hurry to collect his pension money. He got frostbites on his feet and couldn't make it.'

Amy said, 'No one saw him.'

'Now we're getting somewhere,' said Mrs. Mutterance. 'These are good theories. We've got to try to like him. If we like him, even for a short time, we'll find him.'

'But we *don't* like him,' protested Wallace.

'We have to like him,' said Mrs. Mutterance.

'Why, Ma?'

'Because it's Christmas. If we don't find him, we'll lose Christmas.'

'If we do find him we'll lose our shop.'

'Christmas is more important than our shop,' said Mrs. Mutterance. 'And just think if it was you out there, lost in the snow, with the wind blowing down your neck.'

Wallace shivered as he untied his hammock. He said, 'I wouldn't like that.'

'Tomorrow,' said Mrs. Mutterance, 'we'll have a good look.'

The icicles were gone from the eaves the next day, and there were no more ice chunks in the river. The snow was thinner, but it still lay at the edges of the streets, where the ploughs had dumped it, and in the playground and the churchyard. It was messier and darkened by soot, and yet the city still had a magical look. But at breakfast they noticed that the snow was melting. It dripped from the roofs, there was water everywhere, and a great dampness in the air. They suspected that the London snow would be gone before noon.

'We've got to work fast,' said Mrs. Mutterance. 'We'll split up and look for clues, and we'll meet back here at noon.'

Wallace said, 'What about the shop, Ma?'

'I'll have to keep it closed today,' said Mrs. Mutterance. 'I'll lock up.'

'Today's Christmas Eve,' said Wallace. 'This is the

35

busiest day of the year. Everyone wants sweets today—'

'They'll have to buy them at another shop,' said Mrs. Mutterance. 'They'll have to habitate themselves to buying sweets somewhere else. And I'll have to habitate myself to staying closed. So you see, there's no differential in one day. We're going to be closed for good.'

'And all because of Snyder!' said Wallace. Then he smiled and added, 'On the other hand, maybe we won't find him at all.'

They went out. The morning was dark. Fog had gathered in the small square, and the yellow street lamps still burned, giving their muted light to the wet snow and the white-grey fog. Mrs. Mutterance headed for Battersea Bridge once again, Amy walked towards Saint Mary's Church, and Wallace lingered at the shop, watching the mist sifting into the street.

The London snow had come a few days too soon. It should have come on Christmas Eve, while they slept, and showed itself, magically, on Christmas morning. But nothing was right this year. Snyder had given them the news that he was evicting them; and then the snow had come; and then Snyder had disappeared. Now the snow was disappearing, and the city was roughened and bricked-up again, and in a few days they would lose their shop. They searched gloomily in the slush and smoky air, knowing that everything had to change.

The snow had been an interval of enchantment, and it seemed as if it had never really existed; as if, in this wintry city, they had only imagined the two soft days of snow. By noon-time, it had all but gone.

The wet streets were blackened, the roofs still dripped, and the fog enclosing the small square by the riverside shut out the light. It had become what it had always been in winter, a dark city of muffled noises.

Wallace was waiting in the doorway of the shop when Mrs. Mutterance returned.

'Any sign of him?' she asked.

'Only this,' said Wallace. In his hand he held five white teeth fixed to a pink segment of plastic: Snyder's lower denture. 'I found them upstairs. I decided to have another look at the victim's room.'

'He's not a victim yet,' said Mrs. Mutterance. 'Matter of fact, I found out a thing or two. The Chelsea people say he collected his pension. That means he got over there. When I told them he was missing they said I should ring the mortuary.'

'Well?'

'The mortuary don't have anyone who fits his description.' Mrs. Mutterance looked again at the teeth. 'If he left his teeth behind, he must have been in a big hurry. Those teeth prove it. I know that from experience.'

'The snow's gone,' said Wallace. He did not tell Mrs. Mutterance what he saw in his mind: the dead figure of Snyder, from which all the hiding snow had melted, a grey rained-on corpse in a side street. Wallace went on, 'He crossed over to Chelsea. We still don't have any idea where he is now. He must have vanished—and if he has, we're saved.'

'If we don't find him, we're lost,' said Mrs. Mutterance. 'Can you imagine what sort of Christmas we'll have if we can't say to ourselves that we had a good honest look?'

37

'I had a good honest look,' said Wallace, 'and all I found was these choppers.'

'Where's Amy?'

They were still standing in the doorway of the shop, sheltering from the light mist and drizzle that had melted the last of the snow. The city was wet and bleak.

'I haven't seen Amy,' said Wallace.

At that moment, the upper window was thrown open. Amy's white face appeared in the swirling mist.

'I'm up here, Ma,' she said.

'She's inside!' said Mrs. Mutterance. 'What are we going to do? I'm trying my best to find the old sinner and you two aren't doing a thing to help!'

Upstairs, they found Amy huddled at the electric fire. Mrs. Mutterance took off her wet coat and put on a dry one. She sat sadly on a chair and rested her head in her hands. She told Amy how Snyder had been to the pension office, and Wallace showed the teeth he had seen in Snyder's room.

'They're horrid,' said Amy. 'I have the feeling they're going to bite me. Please put them away, Wally.'

'There's no snow left,' said Mrs. Mutterance. 'We don't have a hope of finding him now. We could have tracked him before—but how can we do that now?' She began to sniff.

'Don't cry, Ma,' said Amy.

'He's lost,' said Mrs. Mutterance. 'And we're lost. He'll come back and haunt us.'

'I tracked him,' said Amy. She pointed to Saint Mary's. 'All the way to the churchyard. There were footprints in the snow.'

'But don't you see? It's too late—the footprints are all melted! They've washed into the gutter. Anyway, are you sure they were his footprints?'

'No,' said Amy. 'I wasn't sure.'

'We *are* lost!'

'That's why I saved them,' said Amy.

'Saved what?' said Mrs. Mutterance.

'The footprints,' said Amy.

'I thought you said they were in the snow.'

'They were,' said Amy.

'But the snow's gone! It's unclogulated!'

'The footprints aren't gone. I cut them out. I shovelled them up.' She went to the refrigerator and opened the freezing compartment. 'They're in there.'

There were neat flat parcels, wrapped in foil, in the freezing compartment, like slabs of frozen fish. Amy took them out, and showed one to Mrs. Mutterance. It had a number on it. 'I found this one on Church Road.' She placed it on the table and opened it. 'Yes, this was a good one. I shovelled it up and froze it, then I wrapped it so that it wouldn't get mixed in with the others.'

Mrs. Mutterance was peering over Amy's shoulder. 'It's his!' she said. 'Look, it has a biscuit in the middle of it. That's a holeprint. He has holes in his shoes like this!'

'And this one I found in the churchyard,' said Amy. She unwrapped the second footprint.

'But he couldn't have been in the churchyard,' said Mrs. Mutterance. 'That's not how you get to Chelsea. You go over the bridge to get to Chelsea.'

'This one,' said Amy, unwrapping another, 'I found near the fence.'

'That's his, too—the hole says it all. But what was he doing there?'

'I don't know,' said Amy. 'That's why I brought them back and kept them frozen.'

'Wallace,' said Mrs. Mutterance, 'you're a strong healthy boy, there's no denying that. This little girl hasn't got the strength of a flea. But she's a genius. I tell you, if I had thought a hundred years it wouldn't have occurred to me to freeze a footprint.'

'They would have melted,' said Amy sweetly.

'You used your noddle,' said Mrs. Mutterance proudly. 'Now let's go—I want you to show me exactly where you found these.'

V

A strong wind was blowing across the river, gusting
from the warehouses and factories on the Chelsea
side and stirring the water into brief black fins. The
lighter swung on its barrel mooring as the swift flood-
tide broke against its bow. The weather-vane spun at
the top of Saint Mary's, and the bare trees trembled
in the churchyard. The gravestones were as white as
the snow had been. They were so old most of the
inscriptions had been worn away. They looked like
slabs of chalk, upright in the muddy ground. But it
was a beautiful church, even in this storm. The river
brimmed where the churchyard ended, at the embankment fence.

Amy showed the others where she had found the
first footprint. She led the way, Mrs. Mutterance
questioned her, and Wallace struggled with the stack
of frozen footprints. That first one she placed on the
pavement beside Church Road.

'Which way was it pointing?' asked Mrs. Mutterance.

'To the churchyard,' said Amy.

The footprint, the little slab of snow, became sodden with water and began to fall apart before their eyes.

'Where's the next one to go?' asked Wallace.

'Here,' said Amy. She had marked the spot with a twig. She put the second footprint down in the gravel of the church driveway.

'He must have been going to church! Maybe he's inside!' Mrs. Mutterance was excited. 'He might have taken shelter there from the snow.'

But the twig indicating the next footprint bypassed the church.

'I reckon he could be right around that corner,' said Mrs. Mutterance. She pointed towards the wall of the church where the wind howled.

'I didn't see him,' said Amy.

Wallace widened his eyes and said, 'Maybe he was all covered with snow. Maybe—' But he said nothing more.

Amy was setting down another footprint.

'Are you sure you found one here?' Mrs. Mutterance had become perturbed. She said, 'Oh, bother,' and looked this way and that, into the wind, at the warehouses, the church, the embankment.

'Right here,' said Amy, primly. The snowy footprint unfroze and, receiving the darts of rain, turned grey.

'Where was that man going?' said Mrs. Mutterance.

'I've got one footprint left,' said Wallace.

Amy walked several paces. 'That goes over here,'

she said and pointed her dainty toe at the twig marker. 'This isn't the way to Chelsea,' said Mrs. Mutterance. 'He couldn't have walked along the wall, and he couldn't have taken a short cut through the church. And as for that warehouse,' she went on, gesturing at Silver Belle Flour, 'well, the man can't fly!' She spoke sternly to Amy. 'Honest truly, did you find the footprints here?'

'Honest truly,' said Amy. 'You said we should try to sympathise with Snyder and pretend we were lost. That's what I did. I would come here on a snowy day, because there's a nice weather-vane here on the church, and this is the best view of London. Then I saw the footprints.'

'He came to the church,' said Mrs. Mutterance. 'He must have been lonely. He was walking around in circles, poor old stick.'

'No,' said Amy. 'His feet were pointing in that direction. Into the river.'

Mrs. Mutterance was dripping with rain. It ran off her hat and down her sleeves and fell from her fingers. She said, 'I could do with another footprint.'

Wallace said, 'This is the wrong way to Chelsea.'

'But he got to Chelsea,' said Mrs. Mutterance. 'He collected his pension money. The funny thing is, he didn't make it back.'

Amy said, 'Maybe he took a short cut, Ma.'

'He didn't go that way,' said Mrs. Mutterance, pointing to the Silver Belle Flour warehouse. 'And he didn't go that way,' she said, lifting her dripping mitten to where the embankment ran into The Old Swan tavern. 'And he can't have gone this way.'

She was facing the choppy river. The water slurped

and splashed against the river wall. The river seemed as wide as a lake, and nothing this winter evening moved on it—no boats, no tugs, no rowers. Only chairlegs and branches, and that lighter halfway to the Chelsea shore.

Wallace and Amy also faced the river, but they said nothing.

Mrs. Mutterance said, 'It doesn't seem possible that just two days ago this whole river was solid ice.' Suddenly, she stopped and clutched Wallace's jacket. 'That's it! That's what he did—he walked across the river! He collected his pension. He was in such a hurry to get there, he left his teeth behind.'

'And he was in a hurry to get back,' said Amy.

'To get the rent,' said Wallace. 'So he could kick us out and start his laundry-ette. But he didn't make it.'

'No,' said Mrs. Mutterance, 'because by late afternoon the river wasn't frozen any more. I saw it at six o'clock. It was just icebergs and slosh.'

'We saw it,' said Amy. 'It was half frozen.'

'Cracks,' said Wallace.

'Maybe he fell in,' said Mrs. Mutterance, staring at the turbulent water.

'I'm no dummy,' said Wallace. 'If it was half frozen, then he only got halfway.' He dropped his voice to a whisper. 'Maybe that's how he drowned.'

'Unless he got to safety,' said Mrs. Mutterance.

'This bank is safety,' said Wallace. 'And there weren't any footprints heading home.'

'What about the lighter?' said Mrs. Mutterance, pointing to the dark vessel moored to the barrel in midstream. 'That's just halfway across.'

Amy said, 'He might be inside.'

44

'I can't see a thing,' said Wallace. 'The cabin's dark and it's going up and down. Who wants to swim out and see?'

'You don't have to swim,' said Mrs. Mutterance. 'There's a dinghy in the churchyard and some oars. You're a strong rower, Wally. Now push that boat out.'

Amy said, 'I bet this is the only churchyard in the world that has a dinghy in it.'

The dinghy rested against a tree. Wallace tipped it to the ground and dragged it through the churchyard, zigzagging among the gravestones. He hauled it to a gate in the iron fence, then swung the gate open and launched it.

He said, 'I don't want to go out to that spooky boat alone.'

'We'll all go,' said Mrs. Mutterance.

They got into the dinghy, Amy in the bow, Mrs. Mutterance in the stern, and Wallace sat between them rowing. He struggled against the tide-rip and the stiff wind. The current pulled them down river and almost to the Silver Belle Flour warehouse, but Wallace bravely brought the dinghy around and almost level with the lighter. It was still fifty yards away, but now they could see the name painted on its stern. *Moe*, it said in white paint on the tar-splashed wood.

'I can't see anything yet,' said Amy, whose face was set against the knifing wind.

'I don't want to see anything,' said Wallace.

'Keep rowing, boy!' cried Mrs. Mutterance.

They looked back at the Battersea shore, through the mist and the faint tracings of the tavern and the

45

church, and saw the feeble light, the windows of their own shop. But the rain made it remote, like the friendly buildings in a seaport, becoming dimmer and sadder as the harbour yielded to the open ocean.

Above them were gulls, making for Chelsea.

'They're worried,' said Mrs. Mutterance. 'The storm's getting harrowing.'

'I'm cold,' said Amy.

'Temperature's dropped,' said Mrs. Mutterance. 'Look, the rain's turned to sleet.'

The slivers of ice cascaded upon them and glazed the boards of the dinghy. There were thin shells of it in the river which crumbled like biscuits as Wallace raked the water with his oars.

'We're almost there,' said Mrs. Mutterance. 'Three more strokes, Wally!'

On the third stroke, Wallace swung the dinghy around and grabbed a rope that was dangling from the lighter's deck. He secured the dinghy and then peered over the side and into the porthole of the darkened cabin. By now the sleet was falling fast, and ice covered the lighter from bow to stern.

Wallace said, 'Nothing there.'

'Let's get aboard,' said Mrs. Mutterance.

Wallace scrambled into the lighter and helped Mrs. Mutterance out of the pitching dinghy. Between them, they hoisted Amy into the lighter.

Wallace said, 'This is spooky.'

There were coils of rope on the lighter's deck, and oil drums, and bits of broken machinery. All these were coated in ice. The river beating against the hull made a solemn boom below deck. The wind-driven sleet pattered like sand-grains on the lighter.

'He's not here,' said Wallace.

Amy said, 'I want to go home.'

'He might be inside the cabin,' said Mrs. Mutterance.

'If he is, I don't want to see him,' said Wallace.

'Go and look,' said Mrs. Mutterance, rocking back and forth unsteadily.

Reluctantly, Wallace crept across the slippery deck and along the thwart of the lighter to the cabin door. He got his fingers into the doorframe and pulled. He looked in and gave a low whistle.

'What is it, Wally?'

'There's someone in there,' he said to Mrs. Mutterance, 'but it sure don't look like Snyder.'

'Ask him his name.'

'Don't matter if this man got a name,' said Wallace, putting his big black face above the cabin roof to stare with white eyes at Mrs. Mutterance. 'This man looks dead.'

'I want to go home,' said Amy.

'What was that?' said Mrs. Mutterance.

She had heard a groan, like a bluster of air from a punctured balloon.

'If we don't get out of here quick and call the police, we're going to be in deep trouble,' said Wallace.

The groan came again.

'Help me forward, Wally,' said Mrs. Mutterance, inching towards the cabin on the ice-coated deck. Reaching the cabin door, she stuck her head inside. A large figure was stretched out on the floor, its face turned to the cabin wall. At first glance it looked like a long greasy sack, but Mrs. Mutterance saw a sleeve and a squashed hat and a shoe. The shoe had a hole in it.

'It's him,' said Mrs. Mutterance, breathing hard.

Another groan from the figure: it was weaker now, like air rattling in a narrow pipe.

'Snyder,' called Mrs. Mutterance softly. 'Are you all right?'

The figure rolled over slowly. It was Snyder, his face a strange colour from the pale light that leaked through the porthole.

'Don't hurt me,' he said, in a piteous voice. It was a small voice, smaller than Amy's and full of fear. There was a shiver in it that made it tremble. Snyder's hands were dirty. He clutched his old coat with them and said, 'I've just had a terrible dream.'

'It's me,' said Mrs. Mutterance, and seeing that he had woken and was frightened she became very calm. 'Wally took us for a row. I thought you were probably here.'

'I was trapped,' said Snyder. 'I was crossing the ice. It started to crack. I just made it to this lighter—'

'Oh, sherbet,' said Mrs. Mutterance. She opened her handbag and took out an envelope. 'I thought you might want this.'

'I'm so hungry,' said Snyder. He sat up. 'What's that?'

'Your rent money,' said Mrs. Mutterance.

'Keep it,' he said. He stood up and tottered to the cabin door. There were tears in his eyes as he embraced Mrs. Mutterance. 'I thought I was going to die here. I shouted, but no one heard. Then I was too weak.'

'Look at you—you're all dirty.'

'It's this filthy boat,' said Snyder, whimpering.

'But you'll be all right,' said Mrs. Mutterance.

'You can chuck those clothes into your new laundry-ette and get them nice and clean.'

'No,' said Snyder. 'There's not going to be a laundry-ette, or a washy-teria, or anything. The shop's yours,' he murmured, hugging her again. 'You saved me!'

'If we don't head for shore right now,' said Wallace, 'we're going to have to spend Christmas here.'

'When is Christmas?' asked Snyder.

'Tomorrow,' said Amy, calling from the deck. 'Let's go, Ma. I'm cold!'

'I lost all track of time,' said Snyder. 'I thought I missed Christmas.'

'You didn't miss it,' said Mrs. Mutterance, leading Snyder to the dinghy. 'In fact, you can spend Christmas with us. There won't be much turkey. Just bread and scrape, and plenty of sweets.'

'That reminds me,' said Snyder. 'My teeth—I forgot my teeth.'

'Here,' said Wallace, and took Snyder's teeth out of his pocket.

'What a thoughtful boy,' said Snyder, clapping the teeth into his mouth.

Amy said, 'You're not like Mister Snyder at all.'

'I'm alive,' said Snyder happily. 'It's wonderful to be alive.'

In the dinghy, Mrs. Mutterance said, 'Merry Christmas.'

'And to you, madam,' said Snyder, and kissed her.

'Look!' said Amy.

Wallace paused in his rowing and, as the dinghy turned in the current, they looked up. The lights

49

from Battersea were close but clouded, and the steeple of Saint Mary's was nowhere to be seen. The river was gentler. The wind had dropped.

'I'm saved,' said Snyder.

Mrs. Mutterance said, 'We're all saved.'

It had begun again to snow.